to my nephews

I wish to extend my gratitude to my friends who supported and advised me, without their help I would not be able to complete this book. Nilou Safavieh for the design, Maryam Pirnazar for the edit and Beth Bartholomew for her endless contributions.

ISBN 13: 978-0-9855399-2-4

Published by Zayandeh Publications, New York City

Printed in United Stats of America

ZAYANDEH PUBLICATIONS

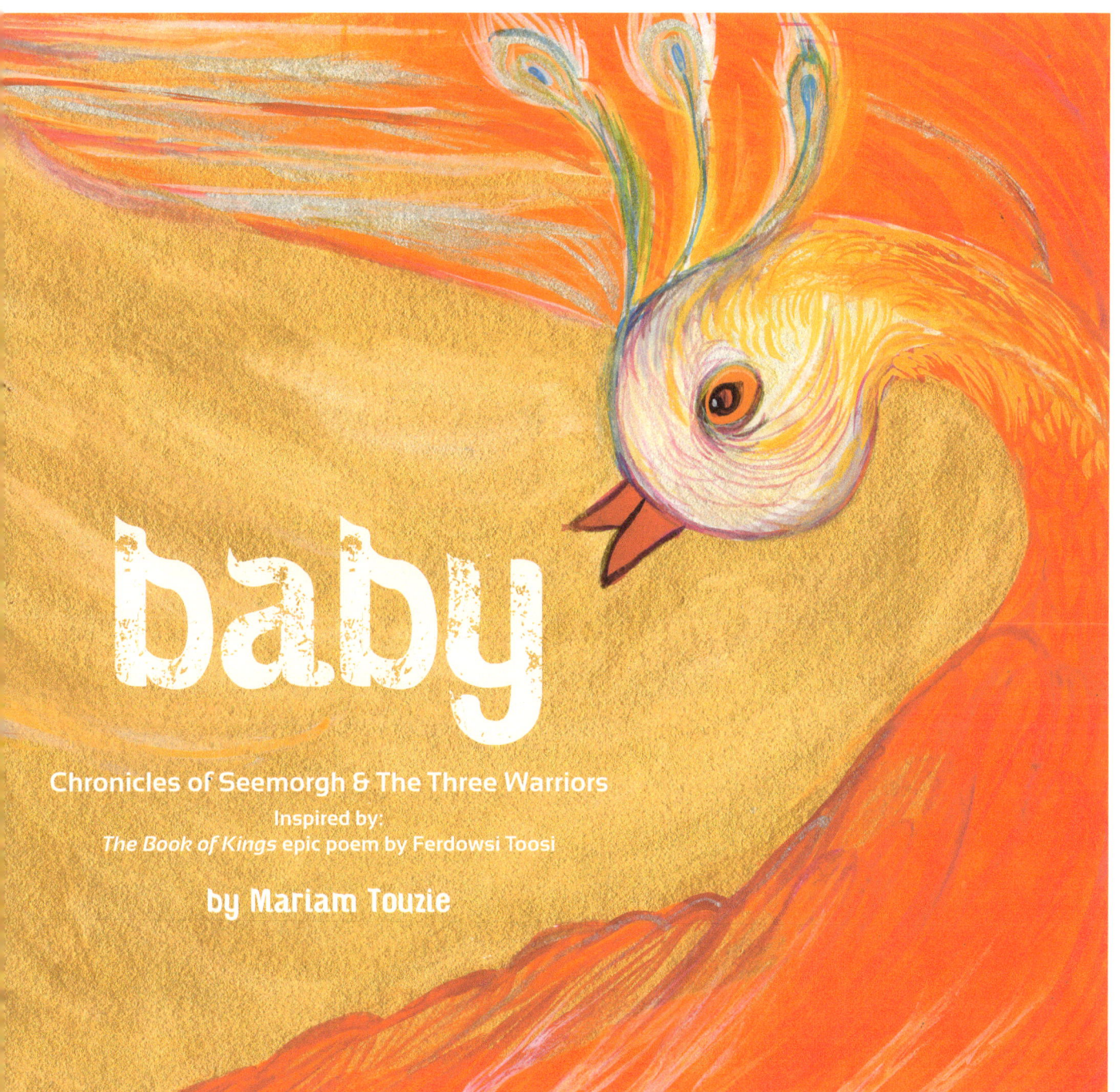

baby

Chronicles of Seemorgh & The Three Warriors

Inspired by:
The Book of Kings epic poem by Ferdowsi Toosi

by Mariam Touzie

"**Baby**" is the story of the child that grew in the womb of Roudabeh, princess of Kabol.

Roudabeh of Kabol marries Zal of Zabolestan despite the bitter history between their homelands.

Zal is the warrior born of a most beautiful woman who dies at childbirth. His father Saum, traumatized by the loss of the love of his life, becomes petrified when faced with his son Zal, a giant albino who resembles neither of his parents. Saum disowns his newborn, abandoning him in the mountains. Seemorgh, the great mythical bird, saves Zal and raises him like one of her own. When the repentant Saum finally comes looking for his son she returns the young boy to the warrior.

Roudabeh, princess of Kabol who inherited the troubled memory of her great, great, great grandfather, marries Zal. The love and marriage of these two young lovers brings everyone to new horizons. The marriage had to be approved not just by the parents of Zal and Roudabeh but also by the King of Zabolestan. Early in his life Zal bravely goes through many tests and trials to gain his place as sage warrior by rising above anger and creating space in his heart for love.

Seemorgh, the mythical bird, is a fascinating presence in the life of Saum the warrior and his son Zal. In this picture book we see the role that she plays in the life of Zal and his family.

These events that took place thousands of years ago in Iran are still inspiring.

✿ Characters in order of appearance ✿

Roudabeh and Zal, the newlyweds

Saum The Warrior, father of Zal

Mehrab, King of Kabol

Ceendokht, Queen of Kabol

King Manoochehr, King of Zabolestan and Iran

The Surgeon

The Midwife

Seemorgh, the mythological bird

Rostam, the baby

The tranquil night at the end of seven days and nights of wedding festivities brings Saum the warrior and his most precious gifts that he had saved for last, to the door of Zal and Roudabeh's new home.

Ceendokht, mother of the bride, is satisfied with the extravagant wedding she had planned for her daughter and is now ready to leave her daughter with Zal. And Mehrab, father of the bride, is still amazed at his capable wife Ceendokht who changed the drums of war to an unforgettable wedding ceremony!

Soon after the wedding Zal receives the King's offerings: Lands to govern and a suitable crown, that are given to him in a ceremonial tradition complete with the court chronicler. Saum the warrior is now the happiest man on earth.

Roudabeh tries to contain herself during the ceremony. In the two weeks since she has learned of her pregnancy she can feel the fetus inside her growing by the minute! In the following weeks Zal needs help to care for the growing baby so he sends for Ceendokht to come and stay by her daughter's bed.

Roudabeh spends most of her pregnancy in bed. In the nine months that she carries the baby her pain increases day by day. On the day of delivery, no midwife, no ointment, nor even the best surgeon can offer any comfort.

The whole household is in turmoil!

In the midst of his desperation Zal remembers the two feathers that Seemorgh had given him years ago. "Seemorgh told me to burn one of her feathers whenever I needed help," Zal says to Ceendokht. "She is the only one that can intervene now!"

Seemorgh appears as soon as Zal sets light to the feather.

"Be calm! Be sure that your child will be born healthy," Seemorgh reassures him.

"And Roudabeh?" Asks the nervous Zal.

"She too will be well. She will forget all this pain the minute she delivers," says Seemorgh. "Now, listen to me and follow my directions."

Zal obeys.

Ceendohht volunteers to harvest the herbs that Seemorgh suggests and prepares them as directed.

Zal is instructed to give Roudabeh as much wine as is necessary to make her unconscious. The next stage is for the surgeon to perform. He must skillfully cut Roudabeh's side to reach the baby. Every step of the way takes place with precise care and Zal uses a Seemorgh feather to apply the paste made from grounded herbs to the wound.

"**Rostam**," Roudabeh names her newborn before falling into a deeply
desired asleep. And the feasts begin everywhere.

Ceendokht kisses the infant Rostam and runs to her husband Mehrab. She wants to be the first to give him the news. She needs to tell him all the details of the fantastic birth so perhaps she can believe them herself!

Zal dispatches messengers of joy to the four corners of the world.

Then with Roudabeh they hire the most elegant tailors to create a liking of Rostam made of the finest fabrics in order to send to Saum the warrior.

aum receives the messenger of Zal and Roudabeh with open arms and says: "If my grandson is as healthy and big as this likeness, then I should give you a gift of your height and weight in gold and precious stones." That makes the messenger rich and happy since he reassures the warrior that the image is true to the dot!

Roudabeh has to hire ten wet nurses to keep up with her son's appetite!

Rostam grows up to be a fine rider before he can walk. He advances day by day as a polo player by practicing daily with his parents.

Finally he is old enough to visit his grandfather Saum.

Rostam and the warrior warm up to each other from the first day. On the second day they plan a hunting trip.

The journey to the wilderness turns out to be the best adventure for everyone.

At sundown they camp. They all relax, cook, eat, drink and talk late into the night.

No one notices the young white elephant who finds wine so delicious that he drinks a whole barrelful!

Rostam hears the ominous sounds of a raucous outside his tent. He peeks through the tent opening and sees the white elephant running every which way, drunk!

gainst all the warnings of his grandfather and friends, and before his grandfather has the chance to stop him, Rostam takes the ancient royal club and waving it runs toward the elephant that is quite crazed by now! With only one blow he knocks the animal flat on the ground to sleep off its drunken adventures.

The event becomes the talk of the town!

Rostam triumphantly returns home after the casual show of his strength with the drunken elephant, still too young to know his own exceptional courage. His father recognizes it and without wasting any time he sends Rostam on his very first mission as a warrior. But before that happens, Rostam has to find a new horse for he is already too heavy to ride even the strongest horse present. The new horse, which he picks out among a huge herd at a ranch raising the very best horses, is the only one that does not let anyone ride her.

"She is a hefty one but has no training," says the owner of the ranch.

"She does not let anyone to even get close to her!" Adds the horse wrangler.

But Rostam has no trouble getting the horse ready for a ride around the ranch at first try!

at day marks the beginning of the
any journeys that will come in the
ars ahead. Rostam and his loyal horse,
khsh, achieve victory in the face of
versity time and time again.

MARIAM TOUZIE

The End

Mariam Touzie was born in Tehran, Iran. She graduated from Tehran University in Fine Arts. She then moved to New York City, continuing her studies at the School of Visual Arts where she received her masters degree and was awarded the Paula Rhodes prize for exquisite artwork.

Her series of illustrated books; "*Chronicles of Seemorgh & The Three Warriors*," consists of three books —"*Birth*," "*Love*," and "*Baby*."

To learn more of her art works please check: www.mariamtouzie.blogspot.com